THE EXPRESS

CARTOONS

FIFTY SECOND SERIES

GILES CHARACTERS™ & © 1998 Express Newspapers plc.

Published by

Pedigree®

BOOKS

The Old Rectory, Matford Lane, Exeter, Devon, EX2 4PS
Under licence from Express Newspapers plc.
Printed in Italy. ISBN 1-874507-20-1

£6.99

GI 52

An Introduction by

John Challis (Boycee)

Giles and his cartoons seem to have been around ever since I became aware that some things were funnier than others. The detail is extravagant. There's always something else to find; a knowing look from a dog, a malevolent child up to no good.

Like the Goon Show, Giles' dysfunctional family changed the face of comedy. It was the first cartoon series that all the family could identify with.
"Look at that mum! See, I'm not bad really, I don't do that!"
"Mum, Vera's just like our Dorothy."
It was for many people their first taste of satire; bringing pithy comment to issues of the day; issues that angered people, bewildered them or just amused.

Like John Sullivan, another writer who has meant a great deal to me and the creator of "Only Fools & Horses", Giles' ability to reach us all makes him part of the very fabric of British life. How many times do we find ourselves saying:
"It's just like a Giles cartoon?"

John Challis

CONTENTS

Christmas

"What happened to your resolution not to set elephant traps for Grandma in 1951?"

"Why, Fingers! We hardly recognised you."

"Grandma – whatever's making you take so long to put pussy out on a cold night like this ?"

"What's to stop the Russians dropping an H-bomb on us and saying it fell from an American plane? Come to that – what's to stop the Americans dropping one on us and saying the Russians dropped it so that they could say it fell from an American plane?"

"So much for your economy plan –
'We'll-go-out-and-get-a-couple-of-pheasants-instead-of-paying-through-the-nose-for-a-turkey.'"

"If he ad-libs once more and says 'How goes it with the Three Wise Guys?'
something's going to happen to that wire"

"Well I **wouldn't** miss the Christmas spirit if I was spending it in the Bahamas."

"Yes, we had a nice Christmas – we all sang carols then Grandma killed off two or three thousand Space Invaders on her video computer"

Social Issues

HERE COMES THE FREEZE
Fuel Crisis brings new emergency
By Walter Terry

ENJOY all the sparkle of the royal wedding today - because afterwards the lights will dim, petrol rationing will loom, coal will be scarce, and the central heating is liable to go off.

On top of all that, money will be tighter, with overdrafts more expensive. And a grim winter of industrial discontent lies ahead for Britain. Unlucky November 13, 1973, will go down in the history of the Heath Government as a day of mishap and humiliation.

As Home Secretary Mr Robert Carr announced a State of Emergency because of a coal and oil shortage, it became a crisis within a crisis for the Government.

1973

Eight Months for a prefab

Prefabs have taken an average of eight to ten months to put up after their sites were handed over. It is disclosed in a White-paper today.

But this month all councils in England and Wales are expected to complete their temporary house building. The last aluminium house should be ready in May.

1948

Army will move food to the shops

Ration breakdown threatens

Express Political Correspondent   Guy Eden

The Cabinet has decided to use troops to get food to the shops and stop a threatened breakdown in rationing.

Government departments reported the breakdown threat to Ministers yesterday - the fourth day of the unofficial transport strikes in London and some provincial towns.

The finely adjusted transport arrangements for rations are not prepared for strike shocks.

1947

More bread if potatoes slump

For some workers says Strachey.

Mr Strachey, The Food Minister, warned yesterday that the potato situation would probably get worse in the late spring, adding: "If it should get sufficiently drastic, and if we were able to, it would be our business to increase the bread allowance to particular categories of consumers".

He told a London meeting of master bakers: "Some factors give grounds for hope that 1948 will not be so difficult as 1947 in the supplies of those materials without which your trade cannot work.

1948

17

"These sex talks in schools have started something – here are more of 'em want to get married."

"How come nobody in this house ever wants to elope?"

"Ask the President to quit playing 'Home on the Range'"

"Here they come, Morgan. Don't forget – sorry we are to be so late, minister's sermon was twice as long this morning."

"Hold it, folks – listen to a recording made a few minutes ago of someone saying:
'Which do you hate most, his summer holiday films or his damn dog doing tricks?'"

"I must remember to have a word with my chauvinist pig about his latest choice in caddies."

"Looks like your kids read that thing this week which said children should be allowed to take up drinking at home."

"Caviar, peacock in aspic, chips, beans and char twice, luv."

"Your punk Sex Pistols are good ambassadors for free speech."

"I know – but it works!"

"This rather alters the tone of my letter to the Express 'Do you love/hate your neighbours' column"

"I've seen it all – howling her eyes out because she's got to go off on holiday without her robot!"

"Madam, I assure you there's no danger of my company folding
and your 7d. a week for the last sixty years going up the spout."

"Any man can be proud to be beaten by his son."

– FASCINATING OPINION ITEM

Fuel Shortages

ON THE ROAD TO RATIONING AS OIL FLOW TIGHTENS UP

By Walter Terry

Petrol rationing could come much earlier than expected, possibly long before Christmas. A crippling cutback in oil from Arab countries makes rationing in some form almost inevitable.

And the only fair way is through coupons with a ration of about 200 miles a month for private motorists.

This was the amount allocated after the 1956 Suez crisis when peacetime fuel rationing had to be imposed for the first time.

1973

WALKER TOPS UP-ON HOPE

Express Political Editor Walter Terry

The Government still hopes to avoid petrol rationing in Britain this winter. And it is banking on three things to bring it off - more help from the Arabs, a return to normal work in the pits, and an end to the top-up-the-tank mania by the motorist.

It is just possible that the gamble could pay off though its prospects at present look slim. Train chaos next week will make things much worse.

But the cabinet is pushing ahead hopefully. Yesterday Mr Peter Walker, the Minister for Trade and Industry, announced new cut-backs to reduce fuel consumption.

1973

E - PETROL COUPONS SOLD TO BLACK MARKET

Ministry man pleads guilty to larceny, forgery, conspiracy

Motorist gave police clue

When the police found a motorist under the influence of drink, they got tracks of "one of the hottest shops" in the black market. "Any thing from a pair of stockings to a battleship" could be bought there, it was said at Manchester Assizes yesterday.

The search, begun when the motorist was found with "E" petrol coupons issued only to those on essential work, led to the appearance in the dock of : - William Ewart Gladstone MacDonald, aged 65, a Ministry of Fuel Officer at St. Annes. Lancs, who pleaded guilty to conspiracy, larceny, forgery and transferring coupons.

1947

"Nip on and tell the Demon King he's had the smoke – we've finished our coal ration."

"Come, Agnes, petrol rationing is not as imminent as all that."

"Mr. Root! Miss Powell! It's not as cold as all that!"

"O.K. fellas, I have apprehended the missing sparklers."

"I'm not hoarding, it's empty, but I like to give the Gestapo next door something to report."

"What would you like with it, luv?
Stamps, wineglasses, tiger tails,
or one on the hooter if you come grovelling round
here once more this week."

"As the Good Book tells us '... he heapeth up riches, and knoweth not who shall gather them'"

"Left foot, then your right foot, there's a good boy! Beastly Arabs, making our poor Algy walk to school."

"Mummy – want to know one reason why Dad's car has been doing more miles to the gallon than yours?"

"You lot aren't here to bring me comfort and joy –
you're here to save your blooming light and heating at home."

"Do you think it would infringe the principles of his three-day week
if he joined our seven-day week and let down a few balloons?"

"NOT IN MY HOUSE YOU DON'T!"

Austerity

"THE KING HAS GLADLY GIVEN CONSENT"
Austerity wedding for Elizabeth
By Guy Eden

A special typewritten addition to the Court Circular, issued from Buckingham Palace this morning, says : "It is with the greatest pleasure that the King and Queen announce the betrothal of their dearly beloved daughter The Princess Elizabeth to Lieutenant Philip Mountbatten R.N., son of the late Prince Andrew of Greece and Princess Andrew (Princess Alice of Battenberg), to which union the King has gladly given his consent"

It is understood that Lieutenant Mountbatten proposed to Princess Elizabeth a week or two ago.

1947

MEAT RATION MENACED BY ROAD STRIKE

Londoners may get no joints

Express Food Reporter KENNETH PIPE

Many parts of London will be seriously short of food if the unofficial strike of 5,000 lorry drivers, which started yesterday, lasts until tomorrow night.

Few shops will be able to supply the meat and bacon rations; there is very little in store.

Billingsgate and Covent Garden are likely to close, because the market traders will not accept delivery of perishable fish and vegetables if they cannot be sure of passing them on in a few hours.

1947

SPARROWS' EGGS ARE VERY TASTY

But don't try to eat the wrens'

By Chapman Pincher

For two years three Cambridge scientists have been eating scrambled eggs without knowing what they were.

It was all part of a test planned by Dr. Hugh B. Cott, to find which wild birds' eggs tasted the best. He published his report today.

He got police permission to collect 81 kinds of eggs. He served them up to Drs. J. Brooks, H.P. Hale and J.R. Hawthorne – but he did not tell them beforehand what sort of eggs he was scrambling.

1948

"That third man in the rear rank there – two paces back and take your greatcoat off."

"And what, may I ask, is the use of my catching the blamed things if you're not going to eat 'em?"

"I met a man who said: 'You want to buy pigs – there'll be money in pigs in a year or two,' he said"

"Just what I expected. Do as Gaitskell says and give 'em lifts
and get yourself pulled for joy riding."

"If Gaitskell does restore the Basic your wonderful home-made self-propelled carriage is going to make us look a pair of d—n fools."

"Think, darling – at last! Just you and I and our own REAL little chair
– our own REAL little table
– a Real little sideboard, maybe…"

"Surely there must be <u>some</u> way of blaming the Russians for this tobacco shortage."

"Break it up, girls – the cops!"

 **Sport**

I SAY BLAME OUR TEST SELECTORS

By Denis Compton

Chairman Alec Bedser and his selectors, Sir Len Hutton, Ken Harrington, Charlie Elliot and skipper Tony Greig, set about picking up the pieces of a shell-shocking England side today. It is a task that will give them plenty of problems — especially now that we are one down with two to play.

But never again must they pursue the stubborn course which ignores new faces for fear of losing. In all my years as a player and reporter I cannot remember a more humiliating defeat than that in the third Test at Old Trafford last week.

1976

BORG COULD BE NO.1 FOR YEARS

TENNIS by Roy McKelvie

Bjorn Borg, 20, and Chris Evert, 21, are the youngest pair of Wimbledon champions for 85 years. Only Wilfred Baddeley and Lottie Dod, both teenagers when they won the titles in 1891, beat them in the record books. Has youth taken over championship tennis? Does this mean that the days of such players as Arthur Ashe, 33, John Newcombe, 33, and Ilie Nastase, 31 are over or that any player in his late twenties is too old?

1976

YOU CAN'T WATCH THE ARSENAL, MASTER SMITH

SCHOOL RULE

From Frank Butler

Four boys of Hounslow College, Middlesex, a secondary school – all in the school football eleven – have been warned that if they continue to attend professional football matches or play in men's teams their parents will be asked to remove them from the school.

1947

57

"You take the bowlers and I'll look after the batting."

"Don't suppose we'll see many men at Lord's while these little lace panties are at Wimbledon."

"Just one thing, fellas – you were supposed to dig this hole two hundred yards down the road."

"If they can lose something the size of Idi Amin,
you're making a lot of fuss about losing two small tickets"

"We appreciate your enthusiastic protest against apartheid Lady,
but the Barbarians are not playing rugby at Lords"

"'Inane looking parrot' is no way to refer to our Ally's national emblem, Grandma"

dear seals,

just a few more lines from me to let you no mr giles is hopping mad. evry morning mr giles is more hopping mad than the day before. he is ever so happy that evryone at home is nice and cold but what makes him wild is because he is nice and cold as well and he says when he was a littel boy at school ~~they tell him africa was as hot as~~ they tell him africa was nice and warm but our littel iland near africa where lord beaverbrooks sends us is about as hot as a fridge. another thing mr giles dont like is the man next door who'se got a camel that keeps scratching itself all night on the wall which is the same wall as mr giles bedroom. he also dont like sand in his wisky and he dont like us putting littel catcusses in his bed for fun and he dont like grandma singing all day with the man who'se got the camel and plays a littel whisle nor do i. mr giles says when it isn't blowing hurry cains its blowing littel locusts in and out his window. aunty vera got sand in her nose and caught a fresh cold and mr giles lands the twins one with a palm tree leaf evry time they call him 'bwana' because he is a white man on account of there not being very much sun. this afternoon mr giles had a go in his jaguar with a italyan man in a ferrari car round the mountains and as mr giles went the fastest the policemen could not catch him but in his mirror he sees them catch the ferrari man and give him a dressing down and this is the first time mr giles laughs since h'es been hear. mrs giles says if mr giles is going to play monty carlo races all over the iland she's going to stay indoors so am i. evrybody here speaks spanish and mr giles is about as hot at spanish as he is at french and when he ordered tea today in spanish the lady slapped his face so he slapped ours. they had a lovely tornardo in the iland next to us so perhaps we shall get one tomorrow hoping this finds you as it leaves me but i doubt it if you knew what the air mail is like from hear yours truly my feet prints pe s. we are all getting as brown as snowballs ➔ ♡♡♡ ♡♡♡♡♡♡ ♡♡

grandma

aunty vera

the twins

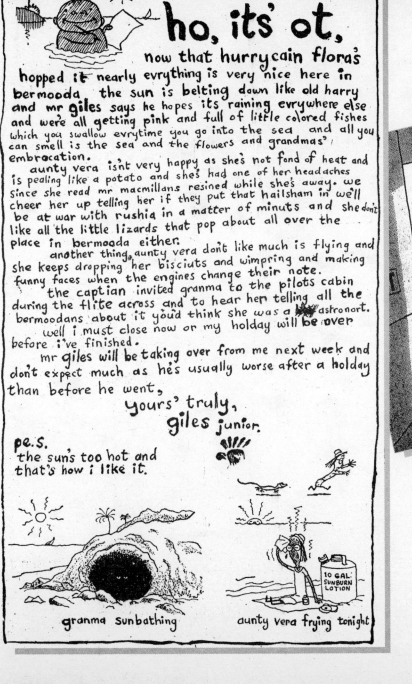

just a few lines

ho, its' ot,

now that hurrycain floras

hopped it nearly evrything is very nice here in bermooda the sun is belting down like old harry and mr giles says he hopes its raining evrywhere else and were all getting pink and full of little colored fishes which you swallow evrytime you go into the sea and all you can smell is the sea and the flowers and grandmas' embrocation.

aunty vera isn't very happy as she's not fond of heat and is pealing like a potato and she's had one of her headaches since she read mr macmillans resined while she's away. we cheer her up telling her if they put that hailsham in we'll be at war with rushia in a matter of minuts and she don't like all the little lizards that pop about all over the place in bermooda either.

another thing aunty vera don't like much is flying and she keeps dropping her bisciuts and wimpring and making funny faces when the engines change their note.

the captian invited granma to the pilots cabin during the flite across and to hear her telling all the bermoodans about it you'd think she was a astronort.

well i must close now or my holday will be over before i've finished.

mr giles will be taking over from me next week and don't expect much as he's usually worse after a holday than before he went,

yours' truly,
giles junior.

pe.s.
the suns too hot and that's how i like it.

granma sunbathing   aunty vera frying tonight

10 GAL. SUNBURN LOTION

I SOLEMNY SWEAR NOT TO "OVERTHRO" THE EXISTING GOVERNMENT OF THE UNITED STATES OF AMERICA

"This is Mr Clever-man's idea – 'Where shall we go this year to get away from it all?'
we asked him. 'Tibet,' he said."

"Oh dear, Rodney is expounding his theory that now we're the United States of Europe all the blighters should learn to speak English."

"What'ya beefing at, Jack – you'd be walking today if you were back at home."

'Whatever will they think of next?'

"Well I DON'T think a nice Sunday walk round the New York Zoo is doing me more good than snoring my head off in an armchair at home."

"I wish you hadn't won two tickets for the Muhammad Ali fight in Kuala Lumpur – we can hear him from back home, anyway."

THE BELOW HAVE ARRIVED ...

A Grandma saying you leave the place for five minutes and up goes the price of her glasses although the last new ones she had was in 1892 and they're not hers. That probably goes for her choppers as well.

B Vera worrying because she'll have to pay more for pills for her nice new rash.

C Dad thinking about Sydney where everybody's got more boats than tea services and they've kicked out the midi.

D Anne thinking it's lovely to be back where she can wear her hideous midi and horrible sexy club boots.

E Bridget thinking the same thing as Dad.

F Mrs. G. being told by policeman that Ernie's been selling bootlegged Australian wines to the children now their free milk is stopped.

G Policeman being told by Mrs. G. Ernie's only been home five minutes.

H Policeman saying that's long enough.

Holidays UK

"Marvellous, isn't it? Come here every year for my holidays
and go back every year telling 'em I've had a wonderful time."

"I suppose this means goodbye to all the little cupboards and sideboards
we were going to build under the 'Do-it-yourself' scheme."

"Want to make holiday headlines? Pick one up in your trunk and fling him over the lion house."

"No use, everybody – we'll have to split up."

The Family, not getting very far with their holiday,
decided to rest awhile to enjoy the natural beauty of the countryside.

"All right – I promise you can ride in the front all the way home.
Now tell me where you've hidden Auntie Vera."

 # Strikes

NOW RAIL CHAOS LOOMS
Strike bid on Monday

Express Industrial Reporter Barrie Devney

Brace yourself as you shiver over the weekend in fuel-starved Britain without petrol for your car to get away... Monday may be tougher because widespread rail stoppages are threatened.

Last night talks between the Railways' Board and train drivers' leaders over new pay demands ended in angry deadlock.

1973

Strike in the West

MINERS GO FOR ALL-OUT WAR

'Stop the lot' plans drawn up

By Barrie Devney

Miners' general Joe Gormley, with a strike set for the weekend, went into action yesterday to halt movement of ALL fuel in Britain and embroil the whole trade union movement in a "short, sharp" battle.

As employers' leader Sir Michael Clapham saw it after talks with Mr. Heath, a strike would be "almost as serious as the outbreak of war".

Like 1972, the miners chief weapon will be picket lines at power stations and oil refineries. Trouble? Mr Gormley said he was warning his men against outsiders "who infiltrate picket lines" and stir things up.

1974

MIDNIGHT - AND ANOTHER 3,900 DECIDE TO JOIN TRANSPORT STRIKES

NEARLY HALF BUSES OFF

One garage votes to go back today

Express Staff Reporter

Another 3,900 drivers and conductors joined the two-day-old London bus strike at midnight. The number out is now 15,700 - more than two in five of all employed.

The new strikers belong to 10 garages. More are holding "shall-we-or-not" meetings.

As the strike snowballed throughout the night it was estimated that there will be no busses on 33 routes and that services will be cut on 61 others. More than 3,260 of Londons 8,900 buses are now standing idle.

"It's Auntie Effie – she says because of the rail strike she, Uncle Jack, Auntie Molly
and the cousins can't come for Whitsun, after all."

"You and your flipping rail strike – lost me me newspaper round – that's what you've done."

"Bus strike or no bus strike I'll get the next lot that take a quick cut
across my garden to the station."

"She says someone has already called and asked them to join the Doctors' Strike.
They had him for lunch."

"As a ship builder I'm on strike, as me own employer I ain't.
Tell your captain I'll do him a refit with pleasure."

"Striking in sympathy with the bus drivers is one thing – refusing to make the tea is another."

"If he doesn't pay me the extra 10/- I'm allowed to earn he's going to have
a wildcat Father Christmas strike on his hands."

"I decided to collect one, miss one, collect one, miss one..."

"Let's get one of these bloody planes in the air and catch up with some sleep"

"Your mother will have to do Manchester and back in better time than that
– we've got Tuesday's papers before yesterday's."

"Do I detect a less fervent support of the train drivers' cause now that he can't get to his team's away match because of no trains on Sunday"

"You've made your blooming minds up too soon! He's not going back till he's finished his ironing."

"Same with mine – 'your boy swallowing a new $\frac{1}{2}$p. does not constitute an emergency.' "

"I assure you there is no question of victimisation because you are Leyland workers
– it's simply that we have sold out of raffle tickets."

"I said it's a good time to get your foot stuck in a chimney with the firemen still out."

"You saw her unprovoked attack and you didn't raise a bloody finger in our defence!"

Anti-Authority Figures

"Dashed good piece of luck, Harry, your second gardener being in hospital same time as you"

"You there! Never mind about how many bicycles it would have made – stick the ------ thing in and let it go."

"Ours not to reason why, mate. Thousands of trendy new ones because the old ones took longer to make a hundred years ago!"

"Go tell your mother I've called from the Ministry to inspect her electric iron."

"Just because we're doing away with your pretty colours,
there's no need to swear like a bargee."

"New list of penalties for civil servants who disclose information about their work.
Done any lately?"

"He's running an exhibition of paintings on the Wild Life of Britain and would like to include one of the Warden who bit the motorist this week."

"Adolf Hitler in the first one, Martin Bormann in the other"

"Fall out, Wilmott."

 # Elections

TORIES IN THE LEAD

Now they're favourites

Daily Express poll of opinion points to a 70 seat majority.

By Ian Aitken

The Tories now lead the Labour Party for the first time in the pre-election popularity race, according to the latest Daily Express Poll of Public Opinion.

A month ago the poll gave Labour a two point lead. This has been transformed into a 2.3-point Tory lead, according to a poll conducted in the closing days of August.

A lead of this size, if it is reflected in the General Election – now practically certain to be held on October 15 – could give Sir Alec Douglas-Home a majority of between 70 and 80 seats, compared with his present 100-odd.

1964

POWER CRISIS GETS WORSE

By Walter Terry

S.O.S warning as steel output staggers

The Hustings echoed again last night to speeches about prices and inflation - but Britain's real crisis kept growing just the same: Industry, starved of coal and steel, is heading fast for shutdown.

"For goodness sake" pleaded Energy Minister Mr Patrick Jenkin, "Let us realise that the consequences of this crisis are desperately serious".

The election hustle, with TV viewing back to normal in the evenings - less electricity is being saved in homes - seemed to have driven the emergency from people's minds. But Mr Jenkin, speaking in his Woodford constituency in Essex gave the real picture.

"Over 80 per cent of industry is on a three day week" he said "Output is down. Exports are being lost. Overseas orders are being cancelled".

1974

ELECTION STRIKE LOOMS

Docks pay talks end in deadlock
by John Grant

October 15 is Polling Day – and could be followed by a dock strike, it was feared last night after talks between employers and unions broke down.

Four hours of argument at the port employers' London headquarters failed to produce compromise. The unions insisted the a 12s.6d-a-week offer was unacceptable. They seek 25s with extras.

1964

109

"I know you want to help daddy's party win the election but you must tell mummy where you've hidden the Conservative candidate."

"I wouldn't be this one – the Tory canvasser called during my Albert's afternoon nap, then the Labour man called and mucked up his tea..."

"Are we sitting comfortably? Then listen to this: Mr Wilson said 'It is the future of the children and the contribution they can make that this election is really about.' "

" 'He is charming, law-abiding, persuasive, a man of great judgement and integrity, trustworthy, and beyond corruption.' So we vote for his opponent."

"As a matter of fact, Madam, I'm not one of your
plaguey party canvassers
– I'm from the Pools to tell you you've come up
with a First Dividend win."

"Squire sure be banging that ball about since he lost his election deposit."

"Awake, beloved, control your feverish impatience to learn the result of last night's voting in the House"

"Lady at the door, Sir. Says she voted for you three days ago
but you still ain't done nothing about raising her pension."

Motoring

HOW TO BEAT POLLUTION - FOR ONLY 50P

I have been testing a revolutionary device. It cuts exhaust pollution and gives a very real saving in petrol and oil consumption.

Call the Scover valve, it was invented and patented by former naval officer Charles Over – a leading authority on hydraulic valves in both industry and the navy.

The gadget is simplicity itself and could cost a mere 50p to produce in volume.

1973

PRESTON
SUPER SPEEDWAY
1 mile ahead
INCREASE SPEED

NO LOITERING
NO STOPPING
NO BREAKDOWNS
NO ANIMALS
NO LEARNERS
NO INVALIDS

HOLD
YOUR
HATS

MOTORING by David Benson

ELEVEN EASY WAYS YOU CAN SAVE PETROL

Everyone's talking about a possible fuel crisis... and how to save petrol should rationing really come about.

So I asked Mobil Oil, organisers of the annual economy run, and among the most experienced people in Britain on fuel-saving driving techniques, for a few tips.

1973

YOUR LIMITS:
50 MPH AND 63 DEGREES
Express Staff Reporter

The Government's shock package of measures yesterday will slow down the motorist and send a chill through every office and factory in the land.

Britain got this message yesterday from Mr. Peter Walker, the Trade and Industry Minister: - The new limit is likely to take effect by the weekend.

STREET LIGHTING will be cut back by half. But exceptions will be made where this could lead to an unacceptably high accident risk.

1973

"But I read the papers yesterday that they let a man off
for playing a mouth-organ while he was driving."

"Oh dear! I've left my reading glasses at home."

"Watch this one, Florrie. It's his fifth blow-out this afternoon."

"Well, so long, Harry – you'll find our insurance in the little tin box
in the cupboard under the stairs."

"Very amusing, sir – it may interest you to know that 1 in 10 failed to read the number and 7 out of 10 have come your old joke and replied: 'What policeman?' "

"Everybody out, Sir, this is as far as we go at 55p a gallon."

Political Comment

U.S. planes blast lairs of Red torpedo boats

MAO TOLD: KEEP OUT!

JOHNSON WARNS AND MOSCOW JOINS IN

From ROSS MARK in Washington
GEOFFREY THURSBY in Hongkong
IAN BRODIE in Moscow

PRESIDENT JOHNSON today followed up the massive American air attacks on the North Vietnam's Red torpedo boats, their bases, and oil supplies with a grim warning directed primarily at Communist China.

The president's warning was: Keep out of the fight.

China is Big Brother to neighbouring North Vietnam - sending her arms and guiding her national policy. For months the Chinese have been building up protective forces near the border.

PRESIDENT JOHNSON issued his warning after it was announced that the U.S. carrier-based planes had smashed 25 of the North's torpedo boats and five of their bases for the loss of two aircraft.

RUSSIA also sounded a warning. At UNO Security Council the Soviet called on America to halt action against North Vietnam "or bear heavy responsibility for the consequences".

RED CHINA, through her official news agency, called the U.S. attack on North Vietnam's torpedo boats and bases "an extremely adventurous action designed to win votes in the coming U.S. presidential election".

1964

NAVY IS TOLD 'SHOOT TO SINK'

From Ross Mark
WASHINGTON, Monday

PRESIDENT JOHNSON today ordered the U.S Navy to destroy any ship which attacks American vessels on the high seas.

U.S officials said one of the three Communist torpedo boats damaged when they attacked the American destroyer Maddox yesterday had apparently sunk. A search today found no trace of it.

President Johnson also ordered U.S warships to continue to patrol off North Vietnam - where the Maddox was attacked - and they will shoot at any challenge from sea or air.

1964

Destroyer in action again
AND SQUADRON JOINS IT IN THREE-HOUR BATTLE WITH TORPEDO BOATS

U.S. FLEET SINKS TWO

From ROSS MARK, Washington, Tuesday

Two Communist torpedo boats were sunk by U.S warships in a new three-hour naval battle off the North Vietnam coast tonight.

Six Russian built torpedo boats attacked the destroyers Maddox and C. Turner Joy in the Gulf of Tonkin in darkness.

The destroyers counter attacked, supported by faster-than-sound Crusader jets from the carriers Ticonderoga and Constellation.

The action was fought 65 miles from the nearest land in 'miserable' weather, says the Defence Department. The American ships and planes were not damaged and there were no American casualties.

The Maddox, which beat off an attack by three North Vietnam torpedo boats last Sunday, had just returned to the Culf with the C. Turner Joy.

The destroyers radioed the carriers for support as soon as the torpedo boats opened fire.

The Ticonderoga, on station 200 miles to the south, and the Constellation, steaming from Hongkong to support her, immediately put up their planes and moved in.

The battle started at about the time that America made public her official protest to North Vietman over the first incident and her warning that there would be "grave consequences" if there were any repetition.

1964

127

"Oh, dear – why do people tuck so many things away in the attic and forget all about them?"

"I expect it's those Tory dockers sabotaging the Communists this time, don't you, Daddy?"

"What's to stop one of them dropping one before our four minute warning system's ready?"

"Cheer up, Vera – America'll soon come up with one bigger than that."

"Now when Ronnie bites his apple I want you all to roll round the room convulsed with laughter, like real M.P.s"

'I ain't heard nothing about a cricket match between Yorkshire and the Vietcong have you Hank?'

 # Topical

MINERS POISED FOR EVEN BIGGER CLAIM

By Don Perry

Even when the coal strike is settled, the ensuing period of peace in the pits may last only seven months. For immense new pay demands ranging from £10 to £20 a week ON TOP of any settlement reached in the present dispute, are now being prepared.

These new claims will be put before the annual conference of the N.U.M at Llandudno in July – *and the militants will demand that the new award be paid as November 1.*

1974

POST OFFICES GET PETROL RATION GUIDE

By Michael Evans

Main post offices throughout the country will receive a top-secret document today with instructions on imminent petrol rationing. Strict orders have been given that the packages are only to be opened by head postmasters. They have already received personal messages warning of the importance of utmost secrecy.

1973

'SAUCER FLEW PAST OUR PLANE'

Express Staff Reporter: Gibraltar. Sunday

Captain Norman Waugh, London ferry pilot who reported seeing a flying saucer over the Bay of Biscay on Friday, said today: "I was flying a Viking bought by the Argentine, and at 10 am, at roughly 8,000 feet, I saw a smudge on the horizon.

"I told the crew – Squadron-Leader Peter Robarts, first officer: Stuart Chinneck, radio operator. We all kept a keen watch. We felt a bit worried at first; then calmed down."

"The object was travelling at lightning speed and looked like a grey tadpole. Within 15 to 20 seconds it passed about 6 miles off. It vanished leaving a long vapour trail".

1947

THE PETROL FIDDLERS FACE JAIL

Express Staff Reporters

JAIL faces anyone breaking new fuel controls proposed by the Government.

The maximum sentence would be three months.

Alternatively there could be a fine not exceeding £400, or both.

The tough measures are outlined in the Fuel and Electricity (Control) Bill which was introduced in the Commons yesterday, and given an unopposed first reading.

1974

"If these people <u>are</u> watching from another world you wouldn't like them to see us
in our last year's hats and costumes, would you, dear?"

"You had no right to let Grandma make you volunteer for ambulance work, Vera."

"Here comes one, lads – seven into 4s. 3d. ....."

"You must explain to Fido in simple doggie language that he's not the only one who's disenchanted with our Government's meat policy."

"When I heard about the £39,000,000 more for farmers I said to myself:
'Alice, my girl – new curtains.' "

"Odd thing – they fly faster than sound but you can still hear them."

"Which do you think we'll get first – 'If-cigarettes-go-up-I'm-giving-up-smoking' or
'If-beer-goes-up-I'm-giving-up-drinking'?"

"Our nuclear alert sure put the clock back in this neck of the woods."

"Bloody fine match this is going to be – rationed to one toilet roll each"

"Dad! Isn't it smashing
– we've got two feet of snow"

"Father, we know the students got their rise
and you're hard up, but we simply
do not want to buy a pig."

"Madam, we could accept your story that your boy painted them but for the coincidence that he has painted exactly one hundred and nineteen."

"Move along there – we've got a customer."

"Why don't you escape, kill a railway guard, make a record, and be a Punk hero overnight?"

"Where'd you read farmers must seek new energy sources
to conserve the fuel we already have?"

"Tell Capt. Hornblower if he buys one, he'll be doing the washing up"

"Off smiles, everyone! National Smile Week is over, in case you didn't know"

"Won't make a lotter difference to Harry who owns the pubs
– he ain't bought a drink since they disbanded the Home Guard."

Family

"What do you mean – they say they needn't go back till next Wednesday?"

"I tell you every year it's a waste of money buying your Mother flowers for Mother's Day."

"Every house has its Lady Falkender running the show."

"Never mind the potted plants – where's me telegram from the Queen?"

155

"In view of the circumstances I think we'll cut cards for who tells Dad
the cat got three of his racing pigeons"

"If we warn them they'll only tell us not to make a noise we'll wake Grandma."

"So much for your 'Let's cut across his bows and get our picture in all the papers.' "

"Wake up dear, 'tis Father's Day. Joint presentation – one jar of tadpoles."

"Reckon we've got a late entry for the Miss World contest tonight
– that's the fourth time she's washed her hair this week"